D0064942

The Boxcar Children® Mysteries

The Boxcar Children
Surprise Island
The Yellow House Mystery
Mystery Ranch
Mike's Mystery
Blue Bay Mystery
The Woodshed Mystery
The Lighthouse Mystery
Mountain Top Mystery
Schoolhouse Mystery
Caboose Mystery
Houseboat Mystery
Snowbound Mystery
Tree House Mystery
Bicycle Mystery
Mystery in the Sand
Mystery Behind the Wall
Bus Station Mystery
Benny Uncovers a Mystery
The Haunted Cabin Mystery
The Deserted Library Mystery
The Animal Shelter Mystery
The Old Motel Mystery
The Mystery of the Hidden Painting
The Amusement Park Mystery
The Mystery of the Mixed-Up Zoo
The Camp Out Mystery
The Mystery Girl
The Mystery Cruise
The Disappearing Friend Mystery
The Mystery of the Singing Ghost
The Mystery in the Snow
The Pizza Mystery
The Mystery Horse
The Mystery at the Dog Show
The Castle Mystery
The Mystery on the Ice
The Mystery of the Lost Village
The Mystery of the Purple Pool
The Ghost Ship Mystery
The Mystery in Washington DC
The Canoe Trip Mystery
The Mystery of the Hidden Beach
The Mystery of the Missing Cat
The Mystery at Snowflake Inn
The Mystery on Stage
The Dinosaur Mystery
The Mystery of the Stolen Music
The Mystery at the Ballpark
The Chocolate Sundae Mystery
The Mystery of the Hot Air Balloon
The Mystery Bookstore
The Pilgrim Village Mystery
The Mystery of the Stolen Boxcar
Mystery in the Cave
The Mystery on the Train
The Mystery at the Fair
The Mystery of the Lost Mine
The Guide Dog Mystery
The Hurricane Mystery

The Pet Shop Mystery
The Mystery of the Secret Message
The Firehouse Mystery
The Mystery in San Francisco
The Niagara Falls Mystery
The Mystery at the Alamo
The Outer Space Mystery
The Soccer Mystery
The Mystery in the Old Attic
The Growling Bear Mystery
The Mystery of the Lake Monster
The Mystery at Peacock Hall
The Windy City Mystery
The Black Pearl Mystery
The Cereal Box Mystery
The Panther Mystery
The Mystery of the Queen's Jewels
The Mystery of the Stolen Sword
The Basketball Mystery
The Movie Star Mystery
The Mystery of the Black Raven
The Mystery of the Pirate's Map
The Ghost Town Mystery
The Mystery in the Mall
The Mystery in New York
The Gymnastics Mystery
The Poison Frog Mystery
The Mystery of the Empty Safe
The Home Run Mystery
The Great Bicycle Race Mystery
The Mystery of the Wild Ponies
The Mystery in the Computer Game
The Honeybee Mystery
The Mystery at the Crooked House
The Hockey Mystery
The Mystery of the Midnight Dog
The Mystery of the Screech Owl
The Summer Camp Mystery
The Copycat Mystery
The Haunted Clock Tower Mystery
The Mystery of the Tiger's Eye
The Disappearing Staircase Mystery
The Mystery on Blizzard Mountain
The Mystery of the Spider's Clue
The Candy Factory Mystery
The Mystery of the Mummy's Curse
The Mystery of the Star Ruby
The Stuffed Bear Mystery
The Mystery of Alligator Swamp
The Mystery at Skeleton Point
The Tattletale Mystery
The Comic Book Mystery

THE COPYCAT MYSTERY

created by

GERTRUDE CHANDLER WARNER

Illustrated by Hodges Soileau

ALBERT WHITMAN & Company
Morton Grove, Illinois

Library of Congress Cataloging-in-Publication Data

Warner, Gertrude Chandler, 1890-1979
The copycat mystery /
created by Gertrude Chandler Warner;
illustrated by Hodges Soileau.
p. cm. — (The boxcar children mysteries)
Summary: A series of practical jokes at a restored nineteenth-century farmhouse makes the Aldens wonder if the ghost of its builder is at work.
ISBN 0-8075-1296-6 (hardcover)
ISBN 0-8075-1297-4 (paperback)
[1. Brothers and sisters—Fiction. 2. Orphans—Fiction.
3. Practical Jokes—Fiction. 4. Mystery and detective stories.]
I. Soileau, Hodges, ill. II. Title.
III. Series: Warner, Gertrude Chandler, 1890-
Boxcar children mysteries.
PZ7.W244 Co 2001 2001017899
[Fic]—dc21 CIP

Published in 2001 by Albert Whitman & Company,
6340 Oakton Street, Morton Grove, Illinois 60053.
Published simultaneously in Canada by
Fitzhenry & Whiteside, Markham, Ontario.
 Printed in the United States of America.
10 9 8 7 6 5 4 3

Cover art by David Cunningham.

Contents

CHAPTER 1

Say Cheese!

"Is that an octopus?" asked six-year-old Benny Alden. "Or a spider?"

"I'll give you a hint," said Mrs. McGregor, the Aldens' housekeeper. She was sitting in an overstuffed chair by the front window, a basket of worn-out clothing at her feet. As she held up her colorful rag creation, eight cloth braids dangled from a roly-poly stuffed head. "The braids are supposed to be arms," she told Benny.

Benny thought for a minute. "A spider

has eight *legs*, and an octopus has eight *arms*. So it must be an octopus!"

"Right!" said Mrs. McGregor. "After I finished the rug for Watch, I decided to use the leftover strips of old clothing to make a pincushion for Madeline. My sister loves to sew as much as I do."

Just then Watch padded his way over to Mrs. McGregor. With a wag of his tail, he licked her hand, making them all laugh.

It was a rainy afternoon and the four Alden children — Henry, Jessie, Violet, and Benny — were sitting cross-legged on the living room floor sorting through a pile of photographs. They were putting together an Alden family album to surprise their grandfather.

"I think Watch is trying to thank you for the rug, Mrs. McGregor," commented fourteen-year-old Henry, the oldest of the Aldens.

Benny nodded. "Watch is very polite."

Their little black-and-white dog pricked up his ears. He wagged his tail again, making them all laugh even harder.

Ten-year-old Violet looked over at their housekeeper. "That's a great way to recycle our old clothing, Mrs. McGregor," she said, pushing up the sleeves of her purple blouse. Purple was Violet's favorite color, and she almost always wore something purple or violet. "I'm sure your sister's going to love that octopus pincushion."

"Just like Watch loves his rag rug," said Jessie, who was two years older than Violet.

Mrs. McGregor seemed pleased. "Do you know why Watch loves that rug? Because it has something from each of the Aldens in it," she said, answering her own question. "And Madeline will love her pincushion for the same reason. After all, it was your teamwork that helped solve a mystery and save our family home from being sold."

"We *are* good detectives," Benny admitted proudly.

"Indeed you are!" said Mrs. McGregor, gazing fondly at each of them.

The children went back to sorting through photos. After a few minutes, Henry said, "Remember this?" He held up a snap-

shot of Benny hugging a rag bear.

Jessie laughed. "How can we ever forget Stockings?"

Benny took the picture from Henry and looked at it closely, smiling a little. "Violet and Jessie made him for me when we were living in the boxcar."

"From a pair of old socks," recalled Violet.

"Sometimes it seems like just yesterday when we were living in the boxcar," remarked Jessie thoughtfully. "Then other times, it feels as if it all happened a very long time ago."

"I know what you mean," said Violet. "A lot has happened since then."

After their parents died, Henry, Jessie, Violet, and Benny had run away together. For a while, they'd made their home in an abandoned boxcar in the woods. They knew they had a grandfather, but they thought he was mean. They soon realized, though, that James Alden wasn't mean at all. When their grandfather invited them to live with him in his big white house in Greenfield, Connecticut, he surprised the children by bringing along the red boxcar, too. Now the boxcar had a very special place in the backyard.

"Some of these pictures are very old," Benny commented.

"Yes, they are," agreed Jessie. She was studying a faded photograph of a lady wearing a high-necked blouse and a long skirt that reached the floor. There was a man in the picture, too. He was dressed in a dark suit and was standing very straight and tall.

"Looks as if some of the photos were taken during the Victorian era," observed Mrs. McGregor.

Benny looked confused. "What's the Victorian era?"

"Those were the years from 1837 to 1901," explained Mrs. McGregor. "The years when Queen Victoria reigned in England."

Benny frowned. "Well, our ancestors from the Victorian era weren't very friendly."

"Why do you say that, Benny?" Henry wanted to know.

"Because nobody's smiling in any of these pictures," Benny replied.

"They do look very serious," admitted Jessie.

Violet spoke up. "There's a good reason for that. You see, it wasn't very easy getting your picture taken in the olden days." Violet knew a lot about photography. It was one of her hobbies, and she often took her camera along when they went on vacation. "People back then had to hold the same pose for almost half an hour."

Benny was surprised. "They had to sit still *that* long?"

"For just one picture?" Henry sounded just as surprised as Benny.

Violet nodded. "And if they moved even a little bit, the picture would turn out all blurry. They even had braces clamped to their necks to keep their heads still."

"No wonder they don't look happy," said Henry. "I bet hardly anybody wanted to get a picture taken back then."

"Oh, but they did!" corrected Violet. "It was actually a very popular thing to do."

Henry's eyebrows shot up. "Really?"

Violet nodded. "During the Civil War, there were even traveling portrait galleries that went from one army camp to another taking pictures. Soldiers liked to send photographs home to their families."

"You sure know a lot about photography, Violet," said Benny with pride in his voice.

"I *do* like reading about it," his sister said, her eyes shining.

Just then the phone rang and Jessie scrambled to her feet to answer it. When she came back a few minutes later, she was shaking her head.

"What's the matter?" Henry wanted to know.

Jessie didn't answer right away. She seemed to be in a daze. Finally she said, "That was the strangest phone call."

"Who was it?" asked Violet, looking at her older sister with concern.

"It was Aunt Jane," replied Jessie. "She

invited us to spend a week with her while Uncle Andy's away on business."

Benny jumped up and clapped his hands. "Yippee!"

"What's strange about that, Jessie?" Violet asked. "Uncle Andy *does* go away on business sometimes."

Jessie nodded. "It's not that," she said. "It's something Aunt Jane said. Something very mysterious."

Benny's eyes widened. "What did she say?"

Jessie sat on the end of the couch. "Aunt Jane said that . . ." She paused as if she couldn't quite believe what she'd heard.

"That what?" asked Henry, urging his sister on.

"That we'd be taking a trip back in time!" finished Jessie.

Confused, the other Aldens looked at one another. Then they all began to speak at once.

"But what did she mean?"

"What else did she say?"

"How can we go back in time?"

Jessie couldn't help laughing as she held up a hand. "Hold on a minute," she said. "I asked Aunt Jane for more details, but she wouldn't say very much about it. Just that it was a surprise."

"That *is* strange," said Violet. "It's not like Aunt Jane to be mysterious."

"No, it's not," agreed Henry.

Mrs. McGregor looked over at them and smiled. "I had a feeling it was only a matter of time before another mystery came along!"

At dinner that evening, the children told their grandfather about the phone call.

"A visit to your aunt Jane is a wonderful idea," said Grandfather Alden as he helped himself to a pork chop. "In fact, I'll drive you to the bus station first thing in the morning if you like."

Kindhearted Violet couldn't help wondering if their grandfather might get lonely without them. "Are you sure you don't mind if we go away?" she asked as she passed the potatoes.

James Alden smiled. "It's been a while since you've seen your aunt Jane. And don't forget, I'll have Watch and Mrs. McGregor to keep me company."

"You'll never guess what, Grandfather!" said Benny. "Aunt Jane says we'll be going back in time."

James Alden chuckled softly. "Sounds like quite an adventure."

"You don't seem surprised, Grandfather," said Henry. "Do you know something about this trip?"

"As a matter of fact I do, Henry. But I don't want to spoil Aunt Jane's surprise."

"Maybe you could give us a hint," suggested Benny.

Grandfather laughed. "Not a chance, Benny! I know what good detectives my grandchildren are. One hint and you'll have it figured out in no time."

"But what do we pack for a trip back in time?" asked Jessie, not really expecting an answer to her question.

Benny looked worried. "On this trip, I *don't* want to get my picture taken."

"Why not, Benny?" Jessie asked in surprise.

"Because I can't sit still that long. Not for that old-fashioned kind of picture."

"Don't worry, Benny," said Violet. "I'll bring my camera along. It's nice and modern."

Benny nodded happily. "I like the quick-as-a-wink kind."

Violet clasped her hands. "This is so exciting! I can hardly wait for tomorrow."

The other Aldens were quick to agree.

The next morning, the skies were clear and the sun was shining. After a breakfast of pancakes, bacon, and bananas, the children hurried upstairs to pack for their trip. At the bus station, they waved good-bye to their grandfather, then filed onto the bus. Jessie and Benny sat together, with Henry and Violet right across the aisle from them.

No sooner had the bus pulled out of the station than Benny said, "I wish I'd eaten one more pancake at breakfast. My stomach's beginning to feel — "

"Empty!" finished Henry, and the others laughed. The youngest Alden was *always* hungry.

"I knew you'd want something to eat before we reached Elmford," Jessie said with a smile. "But I didn't think you'd get hungry *this* soon. Don't worry, though. I packed a little snack."

"Good thinking," said Henry, and Violet nodded. They could always count on Jessie to be organized. She often acted like a mother to her younger brother and sister.

"I brought some plums and peaches," Jessie told them as she reached into her backpack. "And there's a thermos of apple juice in case anybody gets thirsty."

Benny took a bite from one of the juicy plums Jessie handed him. "I wonder what it would be like if we lived in the olden days."

"One thing's for sure," said Henry. "It would take us a lot longer to get to Elmford."

"That's right," agreed Jessie. "There weren't any buses or cars back then."

Violet nodded. "If we lived in the olden

days, we wouldn't be able to visit Aunt Jane very often."

"I wouldn't like that one little bit," said Benny.

Jessie smiled. "No, none of us would like that."

"Things were very different back then," Henry reminded them. "There were no televisions or radios. There wasn't even electricity."

Jessie spoke up. "I know one thing that would be exactly the same in the olden days."

"What's that?" asked Violet.

Jessie grinned. "Certain people would still be hungry all the time!"

At that, even Benny had to laugh.

"I guess some things never change," said Henry.

CHAPTER 2

A Trip Back in Time

When they finally arrived at the Elmford station, Benny was the first to spot Aunt Jane. Bouncing from the bus, he threw his arms around her.

"We're all set for that trip back in time!" he cried.

Aunt Jane laughed as she gave each of the Aldens a warm hug. "Well, let's get your suitcases loaded into the car, and we'll be on our way!"

As they turned onto the highway and left the small town of Elmford behind, Violet rolled down her window. "The country air smells wonderful!" she said.

"Yes," agreed Jessie. "And the farms look so pretty."

When they turned onto the dirt road that led to Aunt Jane's, the car slowed to a stop beside a long gravel driveway lined with trees. Aunt Jane stared out the window, looking bewildered.

"Is anything wrong?" asked Henry, who was sitting up front.

Their aunt pointed to a post at the side of the road. "There's supposed to be a sign hanging from those hooks." After a moment's thought, Aunt Jane shrugged. "I'm sure there's a good reason for it not being there. Now hold on to your seats," she added. "You're about to take that trip back in time!"

The Aldens weren't quite sure what to expect when they drove slowly up the driveway. It wasn't long, though, before a white farmhouse peeked out through the trees and they all drew in their breath.

"Hey!" Benny almost shouted. "That lady

looks like she's from that Victorian era."

It was true. Standing on the front porch of the farmhouse was a fair-haired woman dressed in a high-necked blouse and a long skirt. The children could hardly believe their eyes!

"Good for you, Benny," said Aunt Jane as she parked in front of an old barn. "The lady on the porch *is* supposed to look like someone from that era. As a matter of fact, that happens to be a Victorian farmhouse."

Jessie looked around as they climbed out of the car. "But where in the world are we?"

"This is the old Wagner farm," their aunt told her. "It was built in 1864 by Horace Wagner. His great-great-granddaughter, Elizabeth Pennink, couldn't afford to keep it anymore. So she gave the farm to the town of Elmford to be used as an historic site. The farmhouse has been fixed up to look exactly the way it did when it was first built. And I must say, Carl Mason has done a wonderful job supervising everything."

"Carl Mason?" echoed Henry. "Isn't he

the curator of the Elmford Museum?" The Aldens had met Mr. Mason when they were tracking down their grandmother's stolen necklace.

Aunt Jane nodded. "That's right. Now he's in charge of the Historic Wagner Farmhouse as well."

Benny had a worried look on his face. "Is the lady on the porch . . . a . . . a ghost?"

Aunt Jane gave Benny a hug. "Absolutely not, Benny. That's Gwendolyn Corkum. Carl Mason hired her to keep things running smoothly out here. You see, the farmhouse is finally open to the public this week. Visitors can take guided tours through the house and find out what life was like during the Victorian era."

"Oh!" cried Violet. "That's what you meant about a trip back in time!"

Aunt Jane nodded and smiled. "Eventually, everything will be restored. Even this old pole barn."

As they headed across the lawn toward the farmhouse, Jessie noticed a gray-haired man in overalls weeding the flower beds.

His face was tanned and leathery from the hot sun.

Aunt Jane stopped to introduce the children to Draper Mills, the custodian of the farm. When the Aldens said how do you do, Henry reached out to shake hands. But the elderly man turned away.

Henry and Jessie exchanged a look. Why was the custodian so unfriendly?

"Draper lives right here on the farm," Aunt Jane went on. "He has his own cottage behind the orchard. As you can see, he does a great job of keeping the Victorian gardens looking beautiful."

Draper Mills frowned. "It won't be long before everything's trampled. It's just a matter of time, with so many people coming and going."

Aunt Jane glanced around. "Actually, it looks very quiet and peaceful today. Almost *too* quiet. I'm surprised there aren't *more* visitors."

"Well, I wish there weren't *any* visitors," grumbled Draper. Then he turned and walked away.

"I don't think he likes us very much," said Benny in a small voice.

"Oh, I'm certain he likes you just fine," Aunt Jane assured Benny. "Draper's just shy around people, and that makes him seem a bit grumpy sometimes. He's been running this farm for years, you know. It'll take time for him to get used to all the changes, now that the farm's open to the public." Aunt Jane suddenly clicked her tongue. "Oh, dear!"

Violet asked, "What is it, Aunt Jane?"

"I made a picnic lunch for us, but — "

Benny broke in, "I love picnics!"

"Well, I'm afraid I left the picnic basket in the car, Benny," said Aunt Jane. As she started to walk away, she said over her shoulder, "Why don't you wait here? I'll be right back."

While the Aldens waited, Violet couldn't help noticing that the young woman on the porch seemed rather worried. Gwendolyn Corkum kept running her fingers through her long blond hair and looking around as if she were expecting someone to step out of the house at any moment. And then a small, gray-haired man with a mustache *did* step out of the house.

"Isn't that Carl Mason?" asked Jessie.

Henry nodded. "Yes, and he doesn't look very happy."

A younger man with a camera appeared seconds later. He had dark brown hair and was wearing sunglasses. The sleeves of his white shirt were rolled up above his elbows, and there was a notebook poking up from the back pocket of his pants.

From where they were standing, the Aldens couldn't help overhearing the conversation on the porch.

"I asked Jake North to take some pictures for the Elmford newspaper, Miss Corkum," Carl Mason was saying. "But there isn't a single visitor in sight. I'm afraid we've wasted Mr. North's time today."

"But Mr. Mason, it's — "

The museum curator broke in, "It's not exactly a beehive of activity around here today, is it? I certainly don't want pictures of an empty farmhouse to appear in the paper." Mr. Mason sounded upset. "But what else can be expected without a sign at the entrance? How will anyone know where the farmhouse is located, Miss Corkum?"

"I have no idea what happened to that sign, Mr. Mason," replied the young woman. "It was hanging out front when I arrived this morning."

"You're paid to keep an eye on things around here, Miss Corkum!" Mr. Mason shot back.

Jessie whispered to the others, "That must be the sign Aunt Jane was talking about."

"What could have happened to it?" Violet wondered out loud.

"Maybe it blew away in the wind," Benny said.

"Maybe, Benny," said Jessie. "But I don't think so."

"No, there's hardly any wind at all," Henry pointed out.

Jessie felt uncomfortable listening to the conversation. "Maybe we should walk back to meet Aunt Jane," she suggested in a low voice. "It isn't polite to eavesdrop."

"Good idea," said Violet.

As they headed back across the grass, Henry stopped to look around. "Where's Benny?"

Jessie looked around, too. "He was here a minute ago."

Violet thought for a moment. "Maybe he went to help Aunt Jane."

But Aunt Jane hadn't seen Benny. "He probably just wanted to stretch his legs," she told them.

"Maybe," said Jessie, but she didn't sound so sure.

They decided to split up and look for Benny. Jessie went through the orchard with Aunt Jane, while Henry and Violet checked down by the creek.

"No luck," Henry told them a little later, when he and Violet walked back.

Aunt Jane frowned. "This really *is* getting rather odd."

"Benny can take care of himself, Aunt

Jane," said Henry. "I'm sure there's nothing to worry about." But secretly Henry *was* worried. It wasn't like Benny to wander away without telling them.

Jessie looked worried, too. "Benny couldn't have disappeared into thin air."

All of a sudden Violet cried out, "Look!"

When they turned, they spotted Benny coming out from behind the old pole barn. And he was dragging something behind him.

Jessie was the first to give him a hug. "We were looking everywhere for you."

"How did you get burrs all over your socks?" Violet asked him.

Benny glanced down. "There's lots of weeds behind the barn."

"What in the world were you doing back there?" asked Aunt Jane.

"Looking for the missing sign," replied Benny. "And guess what?" He held up the big sign he'd been dragging behind him. In bright yellow lettering were the words THE HISTORIC WAGNER FARMHOUSE.

THE
HISTORIC
WAGNER
FARM
HOUSE

"Oh, Benny!" Violet clasped her hands. "You found it!"

Mr. Mason looked surprised when Henry and Benny came up the porch steps a few minutes later carrying the sign between them. "Well, if it isn't the Aldens!" he cried. "And Mrs. Bean!"

Gwendolyn Corkum's face broke into a smile. "Oh, you solved the mystery of the missing sign!"

"I'm a very good detective," Benny declared proudly.

The young woman smiled at the four children. "Indeed you are! It just so happens I've heard all about you from your aunt Jane. I'm Gwendolyn Corkum," she added, holding out her hand. "But almost everybody around here calls me Gwen."

The young man with the camera gave them a friendly smile. He took off his sunglasses and reached out to shake hands, too. "Jake North," he said. "I'm a reporter."

"Now, where did you find that sign, Benny?" Mr. Mason wanted to know.

"Hanging on a nail behind the barn," said Benny.

Gwen looked puzzled. "The barn? How did it get there?"

"Must be somebody's idea of a practical joke," guessed Jake. "Trying to be a copycat, no doubt."

"Why do you say that?" Gwen asked.

"Wasn't Horace Wagner a practical joker?" asked Jake. "Maybe somebody's trying to copy him by playing a joke."

Just then a silver-haired lady dressed in Victorian costume stepped out of the house. "Did I hear someone mention practical jokes?" she asked. "You must be talking about Horace Wagner!"

Gwen introduced Elizabeth Pennink, Horace's great-great-granddaughter. "Miss Pennink is one of the volunteers here at the farmhouse," Gwen explained.

"My great-great-grandfather loved practical jokes," Elizabeth Pennink told them. "Maybe it's because he was born on April Fool's Day — born with a twinkle in his eye, I might add! He even got married on April Fool's Day. Of course, Horace's jokes were never meant to hurt anyone," she quickly added. "They were just for fun."

Carl Mason cleared his throat. "Don't let us keep you, Miss Pennink," he said abruptly. "I'm sure you have plenty to keep you busy inside."

"Oh," the older woman said in a quiet voice. "I . . . I didn't mean to go on and on." And with that, she slipped back inside the house.

Violet couldn't understand why Mr. Mason had spoken so sharply. It was clear that Miss Pennink had been hurt by his rudeness.

The museum curator shut the door behind Miss Pennink. "We prefer not to mention Horace Wagner and his practical jokes," he said. "This is a serious project! The important thing is for people to learn what life was like long ago." Carl Mason smoothed his mustache. "Jokes simply do not belong in a museum." Turning to Jake

North, he added, "I trust the newspaper will not mention such silly matters."

"I'll keep that in mind," said Jake.

Mr. Mason nodded. "I'll put the sign back where it belongs on my way out," he said. "And please remember, Miss Corkum," he added, "I'll be out of town for a few days. I hope you'll take your job more seriously while I'm gone."

As Carl Mason went on his way, Jake remarked, "It really is strange, isn't it?"

Henry looked over at him. "What is?"

"That somebody played a practical joke with that sign," answered Jake. "Either there's a copycat joker around here, or . . ."

"Or what?" asked Benny.

Jake said, "Well, let's just say it's enough to make a person believe in ghosts!"

"Ghosts?" cried Benny.

Violet shivered. Was the farm haunted by the ghost of Horace Wagner?

CHAPTER 3

An Offer to Help

Gwen laughed. "As far as I know," she said, "the farmhouse is *not* haunted."

Jake North sighed. "I guess that *would* be hoping for too much."

Jessie caught Henry's eye. Why would anyone *want* a house to be haunted?

"What I mean is, it would make a good newspaper story," Jake said quickly. "Not much happens in a small town like Elmford. The most exciting story I've had to report so far was that they ran out of hot dogs at the local baseball game!"

Benny's big eyes grew even rounder. "They ran out of hot dogs at a baseball game?!"

"You see, Jake?" said Aunt Jane, as everyone laughed. "What *you* don't find interesting, somebody else might."

Violet spoke up shyly. "Grandfather says it's people who make a town interesting."

The young man smiled a little. "I only wish my teachers at college were that easy to please."

Henry looked surprised. "Oh, do you go to college?"

"I'm in the journalism program," Jake told Henry. "I start my second year this fall. My uncle's a writer and a poet. He pulled a few strings and got me a job working for the Elmford newspaper for the summer. It's a chance for me to get some practical experience."

"I *am* sorry we wasted your time today," Gwen said when Jake checked his watch. "But we're having an old-fashioned laundry demonstration tomorrow afternoon. If you could come back, I'm sure you'll be able to take some interesting pictures."

"I'll make a note of it," Jake told her. Then he waved good-bye.

As they watched Jake North drive away in his red sports car, Aunt Jane said, "Would you like to share a picnic lunch with us, Gwen? We'd certainly enjoy your company."

The young woman looked pleased. "Actually, I packed a sandwich today," she said. "But I'd love to join you. I'll just bring my lunch along."

When they were sitting around a picnic table by the creek, Gwen thanked Benny again for finding the missing sign. "You really came to the rescue!" she said.

Benny beamed. "No problem," he said with a grin.

"I love this job," Gwen went on, "but opening week hasn't been easy."

"Has anything else gone wrong?" Violet asked as she helped herself to one of Aunt Jane's delicious egg salad sandwiches.

Gwen took a bite of her sandwich while

she thought about the question. "The truth is," she said at last, "there aren't enough tour guides this week. Too many people went away on family vacations. I'm just grateful for my sister Sharon. And, of course, for Miss Pennink."

Jessie poured some lemonade into Benny's cracked pink cup. He often traveled with the pink cup he'd found while they were living in the boxcar. "What do the volunteers do?" she asked.

Gwen explained, "The museum doesn't have enough money to hire guides, so we rely on volunteers to give the tours. They dress up in Victorian costumes and take visitors through the house, telling them about life in the olden days. It's part of *my* job," she told them, "to train the volunteers and to organize special events at the farmhouse. And, of course, to let people know the museum is open. It certainly doesn't help," she added, "when the farmhouse sign disappears."

Benny looked a bit troubled as he took a bite of his pickle. "There's no such thing as ghosts, right?" he asked, thinking of what Jake had said.

"Don't worry, Benny." Henry put an arm around his brother. "A ghost didn't move that sign."

"But somebody *did* play a practical joke," Benny insisted. "If it wasn't the ghost of Horace Wagner, then who was it?"

Gwen took a sip of lemonade, then she shook her head. "I must admit, it's a mystery."

After lunch, Jessie was anxious to talk to her brothers and sister. "I have an idea," she told them as they tossed paper napkins and watermelon rinds into a nearby trash can. "Can anybody guess what it is?"

Henry said, "You're thinking we could help out at the farmhouse, right?"

"Exactly!" cried Jessie.

Violet seemed surprised. "You mean, as volunteer tour guides?"

"Yes," said Jessie. "It would be fun!"

"It sure would!" agreed Benny.

Henry nodded. "I think that's a terrific idea."

"And we could solve a mystery," added Benny. "The copycat mystery!"

Later, when Gwen heard their offer, her green eyes lit up. "Do you mean it?" she asked as they made their way back to the farmhouse. "I must warn you, it can be hard work."

"Oh, you don't know these children! There's nothing they like better than hard work," said Aunt Jane. "I had a hunch they'd want to help."

"When do we start?" asked Benny, who always got straight to the point.

Gwen laughed. "How does tomorrow sound? I can take you on a tour of the farmhouse right now, if you like."

"We'd like that very much!" replied Jessie, speaking for them all.

As they followed a path through a field of clover, Jessie noticed a small white cottage near the orchard. "That must be where Draper Mills lives," she said to Henry.

Henry nodded. "There he is now, looking out the front window. I think he sees us." When Henry put a hand up to wave, the custodian yanked the curtains closed.

"He isn't very friendly," said Jessie.

"That's for sure," agreed Henry. "I guess we'd better keep out of his way while we're working here."

"Oh, dear!" said Gwen as they came out of the orchard. "It looks like the farmhouse is a lot busier now."

Everyone followed her gaze to where a number of cars were parked.

"Why don't we leave your tour until the morning," she suggested. "That way I can spend more time with you and we can get started on your training."

"We'll be here bright and early," promised Jessie.

As they rounded the farmhouse, Gwen waved to a girl of about fifteen who was standing on the porch talking to an older couple. The young girl looked very much like Gwen. She had the same fair hair and slim build, only she was much taller.

"Oh, it looks like Sharon's back from the dentist," said Gwen. And she waved for her to come over.

When Gwen's sister raised her long skirts above her ankles to come down the porch steps, Violet noticed her socks. They were covered in burrs — just like Benny's.

Sharon gave the Aldens a friendly smile. "Are you here for a tour?" she asked.

"Actually, I'll be taking them on a special tour in the morning," Gwen told her. "You see, the Aldens have offered to help us out this week. Isn't that wonderful? As a matter of fact," she added, "they've already been a help. Benny found the farmhouse sign! The Aldens happen to be first-class detectives."

Sharon's smiled faded. Suddenly she didn't look so friendly. "We don't have time to train new volunteers," she said rather sharply. "Aren't we busy enough as it is?"

The children stared at her in disbelief. Why was Sharon getting upset?

Even Gwen seemed surprised by her sister. "We need all the help we can get. I thought you'd be pleased with such a kind offer."

But Sharon did not look pleased at all.

"They won't even know what to do!" she shot back. "It's just going to be a waste of everybody's time. I mean, what's the point in — "

"Sharon!" Gwen broke in. "What's gotten into you?"

"We'll do a good job," Benny promised. "Just wait and see!"

"And what happened to that reporter?" Sharon asked her sister, changing the subject. "I thought he was going to take pictures of the farmhouse."

"There weren't any visitors," explained Gwen. "Mr. Mason didn't want pictures of an empty farmhouse in the paper."

Sharon frowned, then stormed away.

Gwen apologized for her sister's behavior. "Sharon can be a bit difficult sometimes. But she really has a good heart."

When the Aldens were walking back to the car with Aunt Jane, Henry let out a low whistle. "Gwen's sister sure doesn't want us helping out," he said.

A frown crossed Benny's round face. "It's kind of funny she got so upset."

Jessie didn't think it was funny at all. "Can you believe how rude she was?"

"We *will* do a good job," declared Benny. "Won't we?"

"Sure we will," said Henry. Then he added honestly, "At least, we'll do our best. Nobody can ask more than that."

Violet sighed. She was having second thoughts about working at the farmhouse. What if they had to talk in front of large tour groups?

As if reading her thoughts, Jessie said, "Don't worry, Violet." She knew that her sister was often shy and nervous around strangers. "I'll ask Gwen if we can work together until you feel comfortable."

Violet gave her sister a grateful smile. Jessie always knew just what to say to make her feel better. "Are you sure Gwen won't mind?"

"Gwen will want you to feel comfortable," Aunt Jane assured them.

Benny grinned. "I guess we really *will* find out what it was like in the olden days."

"I think it will be a great experience,"

said Aunt Jane. "And the farmhouse can really use your help."

On the drive to their aunt's, Benny said, "I wonder why Sharon was acting so weird."

Aunt Jane thought about this for a moment. Then she said, "I'm afraid Gwen and her sister don't always see eye to eye."

Benny made a face. "What does *that* mean?"

"It means they don't always get along," Henry told him.

"Oh," said Benny.

"Gwen's been like a mother to Sharon ever since their parents died a few years ago," Aunt Jane explained. "But Sharon's getting older. She wants to do things by herself. I think that causes problems between them sometimes."

The Aldens looked at one another. They were each thinking how lucky they were to get along so well.

Aunt Jane sighed. "It's a shame. Opening week is hard enough for Gwen without Sharon getting upset."

"Well, we can't do anything about

Sharon," Benny put in. "But if that copycat plays any more practical jokes, we'll get to the bottom of it."

"I'm sure you will, Benny," said Aunt Jane. "I'm sure you will."

CHAPTER 4

A Trick of the Eye

The next morning, as soon as they had finished breakfast, the Alden children took the bikes that Aunt Jane kept for them and set off along the quiet country road. A gentle breeze was stirring the long grass and the birds were singing up a storm when they turned off the road onto the tree-lined driveway that led to the Historic Wagner Farmhouse.

"Look!" Benny shouted, pointing to the sign hanging from its post. "It's still right where it belongs."

Henry nodded. "So far, so good."

"I've never been a tour guide before," Benny said excitedly as he walked his bike beside Henry's to the back of the farmhouse.

"It *will* be fun to dress up in Victorian costumes," admitted Violet. She sounded as excited as Benny.

Leaving their bikes behind the old woodshed, they made their way around to the front of the house. When Benny knocked on the door, Jessie looked over at Henry. "Do you think Sharon will be any friendlier today?"

Henry shrugged. "I don't know what to think. But I guess we'll soon find out."

They waited for a moment, then Benny knocked on the door again. "I hope Gwen didn't forget about us," he said, sounding worried.

"Not a chance!" said a voice behind them.

The children whirled around and saw Gwen coming up the porch steps. They hardly recognized her. She was wearing blue track pants and a white T-shirt, and her blond hair was pulled back into a ponytail.

"You haven't been waiting long, have you?" she asked.

"Oh, no," Violet assured her. "We just got here."

Gwen led them along the wraparound porch to the far side of the house. "Let me show you the office first." Unlocking the door, she said, "This is the only room in the house that doesn't look the way it did during the Victorian era. Back then, it was a mudroom — just a place to leave muddy boots and coats. But now it's used as an office and lunchroom."

The children glanced around at what appeared to be a modern kitchen, complete with a refrigerator and stove. In the corner was a desk with a computer, and beside it, a filing cabinet and a bulletin board full of notices.

"As you can see," Gwen went on, "the room's a bit cramped, but it gives me a place to do my paperwork. And it's a quiet spot for the volunteers to come and put their feet up and maybe have a cup of tea. There's a washroom, too, and a little changing room."

Jessie slipped her backpack from her shoulders. "Is it okay if I put our sandwiches in the refrigerator?"

"Sure thing," said Gwen. "I always keep a jug of cold lemonade in there, too. Feel free to help yourselves anytime."

As Jessie put their lunches away, Gwen pointed to the far end of the room. "That door leads directly into the Victorian kitchen," she told them. "But I'd like to take you in the front way. That's where the visitors come in, so you might as well have the same tour you'll be giving them. How does that sound?"

It sounded wonderful. Without wasting another second, the Aldens filed out of the office. As they headed back along the porch, Benny's smile disappeared for a second.

"Do we have to remember everything you tell us?" he asked Gwen.

She shook her head. "All the information's kept in folders in the filing cabinet. You can always brush up on anything you forget."

Benny looked relieved.

"The Victorians liked to impress their visitors," Gwen said as they stepped through the front door. "Especially when they first entered the house."

"It *is* impressive," admitted Jessie, and the others agreed as they gazed around a huge entrance hall with a winding staircase.

Violet, who had brought her camera along, snapped a picture.

"On your right is the parlor," Gwen went on, stepping aside so they could see through the doorway. "It was used on important occasions."

The shadowy room was overflowing with old-fashioned furniture. Portraits in fancy frames covered the walls and the top of the piano, while faded red curtains kept out the morning sun.

"Wow!" said Benny. "There's hardly room to move in there."

Gwen laughed. "To the Victorians, there

was no such thing as *too* much furniture."

"Those chairs don't look very comfortable," said Henry, thinking about the big, cozy chairs in Grandfather's house.

Gwen said, "The parlor shows how prim and proper the Victorians could be. It probably wasn't easy sitting on those stiff-backed chairs for long."

Jessie spoke up. "There wasn't any electricity back in the Victorian era, was there?"

Gwen shook her head. "No, there wasn't, Jessie. They used coal-oil lamps back then. The lamps were usually on all evening and that meant there was a lot of smoke in the rooms. But smoke rises, so the high ceilings helped."

Henry said, "I was wondering why the ceilings were so high."

"Was the smoke from the lamps really that bad?" asked Violet.

"It sure was," replied Gwen. "If the lamps weren't cleaned every day, the smoke around the glass would dim the light."

Just before they went on their way, Gwen

gazed around the room with a troubled look on her face. "I've got the strangest feeling," she said.

"Is anything wrong?" Violet inquired in her gentle voice.

Gwen shrugged a little. "Something just doesn't look quite right in here. But I'm not sure what it is." After one more glance around, she said, "Anyway, let's see the rest of the house, shall we?"

They followed Gwen into the sitting room, where chairs with clawlike feet looked a little more comfortable than the ones in the parlor. Violet guessed from all the books on the shelves that the Victorians must have enjoyed reading. And she was right. Gwen told them the Victorians were very fond of books.

In the dining room, a heavily carved table was set with pretty dishes. The children all agreed that it felt as if Horace and his family might sit down for dinner at any moment!

When Gwen pushed the door of the Victorian kitchen open, she jumped in surprise.

"Oh, Draper!" she cried. "I had no idea you were here. Is anything wrong?"

Draper Mills had suddenly stopped in his tracks halfway across the room. When he saw the Aldens, he looked surprised, then annoyed. "I was, um . . . fixing one of the window shades," he told Gwen in a nervous voice. "But I'll be on my way now." Then, with a few quick strides, he reached the door and was gone.

"That's odd," said Gwen. "I didn't know any of the shades needed fixing." Then she added, "It's a shame Draper's such a shy man. I'm afraid it's difficult for him to be around so many people."

Jessie nodded. "That's what Aunt Jane said." But she couldn't help wondering if it was more than just shyness that had made Draper Mills rush away so quickly.

Gwen pointed out a room just off the kitchen where the laundry was done. "This was called the scullery."

The Aldens looked through the door at

two big tubs on either side of a wooden clothes wringer.

"One tub was used for washing," Gwen went on, "the other for rinsing."

"What's under there?" asked Benny, pointing to where a fancy white tablecloth had been thrown over one of the washtubs.

"Oh, that tub's filled with old clothes," replied Gwen. "We use the clothes in the laundry demonstration."

"What about this room?" asked Benny, peeking into another small room just beside the scullery.

"That's the pantry," explained Gwen. "That's where they kept the flour and sugar and everything else needed for cooking." She glanced around. "I think the kitchen's my favorite room in the house. And that big wood-burning stove over there," she added with a sweep of her hand, "was a very important part of the room. It kept everyone warm and cozy during the cold winters. There's even a water reservoir on the side of the stove. So, the family had hot water for baths and for the laundry and dishes."

Gwen paused. "And see those racks above the stove?"

The Aldens looked up at the wooden poles.

"During the winter," Gwen went on, "the laundry was hung there to dry."

"Stoves sure were important back then," observed Henry.

Gwen smiled. "They were used for a lot more than just cooking."

Benny said, "I bet Mrs. McGregor would like a wood-burning stove."

"Mrs. McGregor's our housekeeper," explained Violet.

After Gwen had taken them upstairs to see the bedrooms, Jessie said, "Thank you. That was a great tour." And the other Aldens echoed her words. The truth was, though, Benny was a little disappointed. He was hoping to hear more about Horace Wagner and his practical jokes.

When they returned to the office, they found Sharon dressed in Victorian costume, sitting at the table holding a small circle of cardboard by two strings. She barely looked up when the Aldens came into the room. She was busy spinning the cardboard circle around and around.

"What *is* that?" Benny asked her.

"A thaumatrope," Sharon mumbled.

"A thauma-*what*?"

"Thaumatrope." Sharon let the cardboard circle slow to a stop. "See? There's a bird on one side and an empty birdcage on the other. Now watch what happens when I twist the string."

Curious, the other Aldens moved closer as the string began to unwind and the circle started to spin.

"Now the bird's *inside* the cage!" cried Benny.

"I bet it's an optical illusion," guessed Jessie.

Henry agreed. "A trick of the eye."

With a slow smile, Sharon explained, "The bird and the cage are spinning so quickly, they look like one picture instead of two. So the bird suddenly looks as if it's inside the cage." She held the thaumatrope out to Benny. "You can have it if you want."

"But it's yours," said Benny.

"That's okay."

"Really?"

"They're easy to make," Sharon said.

Benny was grinning from ear to ear. "Thank you very much."

Sharon was being very nice to Benny, Jessie thought.

Gwen, who had gone to change into her Victorian costume, smiled over at the youngest Alden when she came back into the room. "I'm not surprised you like thaumatropes, Benny," she said. "They were very popular during the Victorian era."

Benny gave the cardboard circle another spin. "I like the way the bird appears inside the cage."

Gwen was putting her track pants and T-shirt into the wardrobe cupboard when she suddenly turned around. "What did you say?"

Benny looked puzzled. "I said, I like the way the bird appears inside the cage."

"Benny!" exclaimed Gwen. "That's it!" And she ran from the room, leaving them all staring after her in amazement. When she came back a few minutes later, she was shaking her head.

"What's going on?" Sharon asked.

"Are you okay?" Jessie inquired at the same time.

Gwen sank down into a chair. She was quiet for a moment. "I knew something wasn't quite right in the parlor," she said at last. "I've been racking my brains trying to figure it out. Thanks to Benny, I finally did."

"*What* did you figure out?" asked Sharon.

"There was an antique birdcage in the parlor," Gwen whispered. "And now it's gone!"

CHAPTER 5

The Copycat Strikes Again

The Aldens were busy helping with tours all morning long. It wasn't until they were having a break for lunch that they could talk about the mystery again.

"You heard what Gwen said this morning," Jessie reminded them as she unwrapped a tuna sandwich. "If the antique birdcage doesn't show up by the end of the day, she'll have no choice but to call the police."

The day was getting hot, and Henry and Benny were barefoot, standing ankle-deep in the creek. Jessie and Violet sat on the grassy bank, their feet dangling in the cool water.

Benny looked worried. "Mr. Mason's not going to be very happy. You don't think Gwen will lose her job, do you?" he asked as Jessie handed him a sandwich. "Mr. Mason was already upset about the farmhouse sign."

"I sure hope not, Benny, but . . ." Jessie stopped and let out a long sigh.

"*But*," finished Henry, "Mr. Mason holds Gwen responsible for what goes on around here."

Jessie nodded slowly. "It sure seems that way."

Violet said, "Why would anyone want to take a birdcage?"

"That *is* strange." Henry held out his cup while Jessie poured lemonade from a thermos. "I have a hunch that whoever took the birdcage probably moved the sign, too."

"I bet the copycat's playing another practical joke," said Benny, who was wading back and forth in the water.

Violet wiggled her toes in the stream. "Well, it isn't very funny," she said. "I'm just glad there wasn't a bird inside the cage."

"Gwen says she's positive the birdcage was in the parlor when she locked up yesterday," Jessie added.

"There wasn't any sign of forced entry," Henry pointed out. "That's why Gwen isn't very eager to call the police. If the house wasn't broken into, it can mean only one thing."

The other Aldens knew what Henry was going to say. It had to be someone who had keys to the farmhouse. But who was that someone? And was this another practical joke like the ones Horace Wagner had played so long ago?

The children were quiet as they finished their lunch of sandwiches, chips, and fresh fruit. They had plenty of questions. The problem was, they didn't have any answers. Finally, Henry looked at his watch. "We promised we'd help with the laundry demonstration."

"Right," said Jessie as Violet took a quick picture of Henry and Benny. "I guess we should be going."

They were making their way through the long grass when they spotted Miss Pennink gathering wildflowers. She gave the Aldens a warm smile.

"What a charming picture you make in those old-fashioned clothes!" she said. "By the way," she added, "how do those pants feel, Benny?"

"They feel just right!" Benny told her, with a nod and a grin. "Thanks for making them shorter, Miss Pennink."

"Well, we can't have our guides tripping over their pant legs," said Miss Pennink as she fell into step beside them. "Isn't it a beautiful day to be out in the country?" she added.

The Aldens were quick to agree. "Do you miss living out here, Miss Pennink?" Violet wondered.

"Oh, yes," she replied. "Of course, I have a very nice little house in town. And it *does* have a bit of a backyard. But this farm still feels like home to me. It does my heart good, though, to see the old place restored.

"Draper, of course, did his best to keep the house from completely falling apart," she went on. "But the truth is, I didn't have enough money to pay for all the work that needed to be done. Now, thanks to the museum, the farmhouse looks just as wonderful as it did before the days of electricity and indoor plumbing."

"Our boxcar didn't have electricity, either," Benny commented. "Or running water. And you know what else? We even cooked over an open fire!"

After the Aldens took turns telling Miss Pennink all about their boxcar days, she shook her head in amazement. "What smart children you are!" she exclaimed. "And maybe you didn't have electricity or running water, but you had something else."

They turned to look at her.

"You had one another," she told them. "And that's more important than anything else."

The Aldens knew it was true, and they

exchanged happy glances. "Now we have Grandfather, too," Violet said in a soft voice.

"Don't forget about Mrs. McGregor and Watch," Benny added. "Their pictures are in the Alden family album, too."

Miss Pennink suddenly lowered her voice. "There used to be a picture of my great-great-grandfather in the parlor of the farmhouse," she said.

Henry looked puzzled. "*Used* to be?"

Miss Pennink leaned closer and whispered, "Carl Mason had it removed!"

The Aldens were surprised to hear this. "Why did he do that?" asked Benny.

"Because Carl Mason has no sense of humor whatsoever!" cried Miss Pennink. No sooner had the words escaped than she clapped a hand over her mouth. "Oh, I didn't mean to say that. It just upsets me that Mr. Mason wants the world to . . . well, to forget all about Horace Wagner!"

"Your great-great-grandfather's picture was actually removed from the parlor?" Jessie said, finding it hard to believe.

"The farmhouse wouldn't even be here if it wasn't for Horace Wagner!" Violet pointed out.

Miss Pennink nodded. "I suppose Mr. Mason was afraid it would raise a few questions about Horace and his practical jokes. From visitors, I mean."

"Why would anyone ask about his practical jokes," Henry wanted to know, "just because of a photograph?"

"Because Horace could *never* resist a practical joke," Miss Pennink explained, smiling a little. "Not even when he was being photographed."

The children stared wide-eyed at Miss Pennink. "What do you mean?"

Miss Pennink's voice was hushed. "In the photograph, Horace has a flower tucked behind his ear!"

Henry, Jessie, Violet, and Benny looked at one another and began to laugh.

Miss Pennink laughed, too, as they continued through the orchard. "That portrait really *is* the funniest thing!" she said. "Horace looks so solemn and stern, but he has this silly flower that ought to be in his buttonhole — "

"Stuck behind his ear!" finished Benny. He liked Horace Wagner!

"I'd like to see that photograph!" said Henry.

Violet was still giggling. "Your great-great-grandfather sure wasn't a prim and proper Victorian, Miss Pennink."

"No, indeed!" agreed Miss Pennink. "And one way or another, I intend to make sure everyone knows it!" With that, she marched up the porch steps and disappeared into the farmhouse.

The Aldens exchanged puzzled looks. What did Miss Pennink mean by *one way or another*?

They had little time to think about it, though. When they stepped into the Victorian kitchen, they caught sight of Sharon holding up an antique birdcage!

Gwen was shaking her head in bewilderment. "I can't believe it! How in the world did a bird get inside that cage?"

The Aldens looked closer. Sure enough,

a little yellow canary was flitting from perch to perch!

Benny's eyes were huge. "Is that another optical illusion?"

Sharon shook her head, looking pleased. "No way!"

"Where *exactly* did you find the missing birdcage, Sharon?" inquired Gwen.

"In the scullery," Sharon told her sister as she set the birdcage down on the kitchen table. "You know that old lace tablecloth that was over one of the tubs? Well, the cage was hidden underneath."

Puzzled, Jessie said, "I thought you looked in the scullery this morning."

Sharon seemed annoyed by Jessie's question. "I didn't check under the tablecloth. I thought there were only old clothes underneath. It wasn't until I started getting things ready for the laundry demonstration that I noticed the birdcage."

"I know it was in the parlor yesterday," said Gwen. "Without the canary!"

"Looks like somebody's playing practical jokes again," said Jake North.

The Aldens turned around in surprise. They hadn't noticed the reporter standing in a corner of the kitchen.

"That's exactly what it looks like," said Miss Pennink, slumping down into a chair.

Gwen placed a gentle hand on the elderly woman's shoulder. "Are you all right, Miss Pennink?" she asked.

"I heard so many stories about Horace when I was growing up," said Miss Pennink. "The birdcage-in-the-laundry-tub was one of those stories."

Curious, everyone moved closer to hear what Miss Pennink had to say.

"According to the story," said Miss Pennink, "Amanda Wagner — Horace's wife — dreaded doing the laundry and always said she wished it would just sprout wings and fly away."

"I've heard it was hard work in those days," commented Jake.

Miss Pennink nodded. "Horace wanted it to seem as if the laundry really *had* sprouted wings. So, on one of his business trips, he bought an anniversary gift for his wife — a birdcage with a little yellow canary inside." Miss Pennink paused. "Then, on April Fool's Day, he hid the birdcage in an empty laundry tub in the scullery. They say that Amanda was just delighted when she found it there."

Gwen stared at the canary in the cage. "Then this is an *exact* copy of that practical joke?"

Miss Pennink nodded slowly. "Horace did this so people would notice him. He doesn't like to be forgotten in his own home."

Jessie felt a chill up her spine. She didn't really believe in ghosts, but she couldn't help wondering if the ghost of Horace Wagner *was* responsible for the practical jokes.

They had to put all thoughts of the mystery aside for a while as visitors started arriving. Gwen took the birdcage into the back office, while the Aldens helped Sharon carry the washtubs and wringers out to the side porch for the laundry demonstration.

Jake took photographs while they filled the washtubs with water from the pump. And when enough visitors had gathered on the porch, Sharon began the demonstration. She showed everyone how the clothes were scrubbed against a washboard to get them clean, then put through the wooden rollers to squeeze the water out. With Henry's help, Benny turned the crank on the wringer around and around.

Later, Gwen stuck her head out the door and offered Jake a cup of coffee.

"Sounds great!" Jake said as he put the cap back on the lens of the camera. "I was just finishing up here anyway." Before he went inside, he stopped to whisper to the Aldens, "Sure hope I don't see any ghosts lurking in the background when these pictures are developed."

When he was gone, Violet said, "I've got goose bumps just thinking about it."

"I don't understand it," said Henry, keeping his voice low. "Somebody's going to a lot of trouble to make everyone think the farmhouse is haunted."

"You're right, Henry," agreed Jessie. "But it's a mystery why anyone would want to do such a thing."

It *was* a mystery — but it was a mystery the Aldens were determined to solve.

CHAPTER 6

Aunt Jane's Treat

Benny was tearing the lettuce into bite-sized pieces for dinner. "Working as a tour guide sure gives me an appetite!" he said.

"*Everything* gives you an appetite, Benny." Henry laughed as he took a wooden salad bowl down from the cupboard and handed it to his younger brother.

After returning from the Wagner farm, the Aldens had gone for a quick dip in the pond near their aunt's house. Now, cool and refreshed, they were busy helping with dinner.

"I just can't believe it!" said Aunt Jane, who still hadn't gotten over the shock after hearing about the latest practical joke. "There was actually a *canary* inside the birdcage?"

Jessie nodded as she sliced cucumbers for the salad. "Gwen said the canary couldn't stay in the farmhouse, so Miss Pennink took the little bird home with her."

"Miss Pennink plans to bring the antique cage back in the morning," added Henry as he carefully chopped up carrots and celery. "She's going to buy a new birdcage for Nester."

Aunt Jane raised an eyebrow. "Is that the canary's name?"

Benny was washing a handful of cherry tomatoes under the tap. "Nester's a very good name for a canary. Don't you think so, Aunt Jane?"

Aunt Jane smiled at Benny. "Absolutely! After all, birds *do* make nests," she said.

"Was that name, by any chance, *your* idea, Benny?"

The youngest Alden beamed proudly. "How'd you guess?"

"Oh, just a hunch." Aunt Jane's eyes twinkled.

Jessie couldn't help noticing that her sister was unusually quiet. "Is anything wrong, Violet?"

"Not really." Violet added another spoonful of mayonnaise to the potato salad, then smiled a little at Jessie. "I just can't get the copycat off my mind."

Henry looked over at her as he put a basket of rolls and a dish of homemade pickles on the table. "Do you think you know who it is, Violet?"

She shook her head. "No. But this person, whoever it is, sure knows a lot about Horace Wagner."

"That's true," said Henry. "He or she knows a lot about Horace *and* his practical jokes."

"Your first day on the job," Aunt Jane

said when they finally sat down at the table, "and already you're knee-deep in a mystery."

Benny grinned. "Grandfather says we attract mysteries the way a magnet attracts iron."

"I'll second that!" said Aunt Jane. Then a frown crossed her kind face. "I just hope you don't get in over your heads."

"Don't worry, Aunt Jane," said Jessie. "We'll look out for one another."

Aunt Jane smiled. "I know you will. That's one thing I can always count on."

Henry spoke up. "Aunt Jane, you said that Draper Mills has been running the farm for a long time, right?"

Aunt Jane nodded. "Ever since he was a young man. Most of the poetry he writes is about farm life. Draper's an excellent poet, you know. He wrote a book of poetry called *Where the Buttercups Grow.* I believe Draper Mills loves that farm every bit as much as Miss Pennink does." Aunt Jane paused for a moment. "In his heart, I think he's glad to see it restored, thanks to Carl Mason."

"I know one thing," said Benny as he passed the rolls. "Mr. Mason sure isn't the copycat!"

Henry lifted a slice of cold chicken onto his plate. "That's true, Benny. Mr. Mason made it clear he doesn't like jokes in the museum!"

Aunt Jane put down her fork. "Carl Mason does a good job, but I'm afraid I don't share his views on everything. People often think of museums as boring and stuffy. Carl Mason's prim and proper attitude isn't going to do much to change that."

"It's funny that Horace *wasn't* prim and proper," Violet said, "even though he lived in the Victorian era. But Mr. Mason *is* prim and proper, and he *doesn't* live in the Victorian era."

Aunt Jane nodded. "It doesn't make sense, does it? It's almost as if some people were born in the wrong century."

They grew quiet as they feasted on their delicious dinner. But when Benny started to pile his plate a second time, Aunt Jane spoke up. "Don't forget to leave room for dessert," she said. "It just so happens, we're having something very special tonight."

Benny's eyes lit up. "Something special?"

Aunt Jane nodded as she took a sip of her iced tea. "A new ice-cream parlor just opened up in town. I thought we might give it a try. What do you think?"

Everyone thought it was a great idea. As they cleared the table, Henry had an idea, too. "When we're in town," he told them, "we can check out the pet store."

Handing Benny more dishes, Violet gave Henry a confused look. "The pet store?"

"I think I know why," said Jessie, who was standing at the sink, up to her elbows in soapsuds. "To find out if someone bought a canary recently. Right, Henry?"

"Oh," exclaimed Violet. "I hadn't thought of that."

"It's worth a shot," said Henry as he reached for a dish towel.

Benny was grinning from ear to ear. "I bet we find out who the copycat is in no time flat!"

"I hope so, Benny," said Henry. "I hope so."

Aunt Jane and the four children sat down together in an empty booth near the window of Elmford's new ice-cream parlor after dropping Violet's film off at the one-hour photo shop.

"It certainly is busy in here," commented Jessie as she glanced around at the crowded room with its decorations of brightly colored streamers and balloons.

Aunt Jane ran her hand admiringly over the soft, lavender-colored seats. "There's a two-for-one special going on all week. It's bound to attract customers."

"Who'd want to pass up a deal like that?" exclaimed Henry as he opened a menu and glanced down at the long list of selections.

It only took them a few minutes to decide what they wanted. Their order included a banana split for Henry, a waffle cone with two scoops of black cherry ice cream for Jessie, a chocolate sundae with extra chocolate sprinkles for Benny, and strawberry milk shakes for Violet and Aunt Jane.

When the waiter brought their ice cream, Benny didn't waste any time before digging right in. "Thanks, Aunt Jane," he said. "This was a great idea."

The other Aldens nodded in agreement. "It's a perfect way to end the day," said Jessie as she handed everyone a napkin from the shiny new dispenser.

Aunt Jane looked pleased. "It's a well-deserved treat," she said. "Sounds as if you had a very busy day at the farmhouse."

"Well, we did spend all afternoon helping with the laundry demonstration," Henry said.

Jessie nodded. "Now I know why Amanda Wagner didn't like *that* chore!"

"Yes," said Violet. "It really was hard work in the olden days."

"They even had *unhappy* irons in the Victorian era!" added Benny.

"Oh, Benny!" Jessie ruffled her younger brother's hair. "They're called *sad*irons. Re-

member, Gwen told us *sad* can also mean *heavy*."

Aunt Jane nodded. "I've heard some of those sadirons weighed as much as fifteen pounds."

Suddenly familiar voices interrupted their conversation. When they looked over, they spotted Gwen and Sharon sitting at another booth. Sharon's face was flushed, and her voice was raised in anger. Aunt Jane and the children didn't mean to eavesdrop, but they couldn't help overhearing. The two sisters were almost shouting.

"You never listen, Gwen! I'm not interested in the same things you are! Why can't you understand that?"

"I'm not going to sit back and let you make foolish choices," replied Gwen. "You'll thank me for it one day."

"No, I won't! I won't thank you for ruining my life!"

"Oh, Sharon! Your life won't be ruined just because you don't take part in those silly fashion shows. You'll be busy with your studies when school starts again. I don't want you spending your weekends modeling when — "

Sharon suddenly leaped to her feet. "What about what I want? You're not being fair!"

Gwen looked as if she wanted to argue, but she didn't. Instead, she just sat quietly while Sharon stormed out of the ice-cream parlor.

"Wow," Henry whispered. "You weren't kidding, Aunt Jane! Gwen and Sharon really don't see eye to eye. Now they're arguing about modeling."

"I think Sharon's a born model," remarked Jessie, remembering how Gwen's younger sister had somehow managed to get into every picture Jake North had taken during the laundry demonstration.

"Just like Benny's a born ice-cream eater!" teased Henry as he watched his brother scraping chocolate sauce from the bottom of his dish.

Benny gave him the thumbs-up sign. "Right!"

Soon they were done and ready to head

for the pet store. Leaving Aunt Jane to keep Gwen company, the Aldens hurried outside. They decided to make a stop at the photo shop on the way to pick up Violet's pictures.

While Violet stood in line, Jessie noticed a poster on the wall. It was an advertisement for fashion shows that were to take place at a local mall all summer and fall. Jessie motioned toward the poster. "I wonder if that's what Gwen and Sharon were arguing about," she said.

Henry studied the poster for a moment. "It *does* say they need people to model clothes. And did you notice the fine print?" Henry ran a finger under the words at the bottom of the poster. " 'Anyone under the age of sixteen will need written permission from a parent or guardian before taking part in the shows.' "

"Sharon's only fifteen, isn't she?" Benny asked when they came out of the photo shop.

Jessie nodded. "And from what we heard, I doubt Gwen's going to give Sharon permission."

"I wonder if Sharon likes modeling as

much as I like drawing," Violet said. Though Violet thought it was rude of Gwen's sister to storm out of the ice-cream parlor, she couldn't help feeling a bit sorry for her. It would be hard if you couldn't do something you really enjoyed.

"That doesn't excuse Sharon for being rude to Gwen," Jessie said, walking into the pet store.

The man behind the counter looked up from his book when the Aldens approached. "Hello there," he said.

"Hi," responded Benny. "Have you sold any canaries lately?"

The other Aldens exchanged smiles. They could always count on Benny not to waste time on small talk.

The man removed his wire-rimmed glasses and shook his head. "We don't sell canaries here. But we do have a couple of parakeets, if you're interested."

"No, thanks," said Benny.

Outside, the Aldens turned to one another in dismay. "Looks like we struck out," Henry couldn't help saying.

On the drive back to Aunt Jane's, Jessie said, "You know, even if that store *did* sell canaries, the copycat might not have been foolish enough to buy one right here in Elmford."

Henry was forced to agree. "Yes, that's a sure way to get found out in no time." He looked a bit sheepish as he glanced back over his shoulder at his brother and sisters. "I guess I didn't give it much thought."

"It was worth a try," insisted Violet as she looked through her snapshots. There was one of Gwen standing in the shadowy parlor that wasn't very clear. And another one taken down by the creek that was a bit blurry. But most of them had turned out just fine. "This one is very nice," Violet commented.

"Which one is that?" asked Jessie, looking over.

"The one Gwen took of us standing in the office," replied Violet, passing the snapshot to her older sister, "when we were still in our costumes."

"Oh, that was just after we finished the

laundry demonstration," said Jessie as she had a turn flipping through some of the photographs. "This one of Miss Pennink sitting on the porch is good, too," she said. "You're a terrific photographer, Violet!"

"Miss Pennink deserves the credit," Violet said modestly. "She has such a beautiful face. The camera loves her."

As they were nearing the old Wagner farm, Benny suddenly cried, "Look, isn't that Jake's car?"

Sure enough, a little red sports car pulled out of the driveway onto the dirt road. Benny raised a hand to wave, but Jake passed by without noticing them.

"What's Jake doing here again?" Violet wondered aloud.

Then Jessie added another question. "And why is he here so late at night?"

"Do you think he was coming to do a copycat trick?" Benny asked.

"Maybe we shouldn't be too hasty," Henry broke in. "There might be a very good reason for Jake being at the farmhouse. It doesn't necessarily make him a suspect."

"You're right, Henry," said Violet. "We shouldn't jump to any conclusions."

Aunt Jane was quick to agree. "Sometimes the Elmford newspaper runs a color picture on the front page of its weekend edition," she told them. "Maybe Jake wanted to photograph the farmhouse at sunset."

Benny sighed. "This is going to be a tough mystery to solve!"

Jessie put an arm around her younger brother. "It might take us a bit of time, but we *will* get to the bottom of this," she said encouragingly. "Isn't solving mysteries our specialty?"

Benny nodded. "We *are* good detectives."

"And we can't let Gwen lose her job," added Henry.

Violet spoke up hopefully. "Who knows? Maybe the copycat won't bother playing any more practical jokes."

"Maybe," said Jessie. But none of them believed it for a minute.

CHAPTER 7

The Double Take

The next morning, Benny stepped out of the changing room and announced, "I'm growing like a weed!"

Violet looked over at Benny. "What in the world . . . ?"

"What happened?" asked Jessie.

Benny scratched his head. "I guess I sprouted up last night."

Sure enough, Benny's pants were now at least five inches too short.

"I think you've got the wrong pants on, Benny," Violet guessed.

Jessie nodded. "Those are *way* too short."

Benny shook his head. "See?" He reached into his pocket and pulled out the thaumatrope Sharon had given him. "These *are* my pants. I put this in my pocket yesterday."

When Henry came into the room, everyone cried out in surprise. Benny wasn't the only one wearing pants that were too short!

"What . . . ?" Benny couldn't believe his eyes.

For a long moment, the two brothers stood staring at each other. Then they suddenly burst into laughter.

"We sure look funny!" Benny exclaimed.

"You can say that again!" admitted Henry, looking down at his own too-short pants.

"Hmmm." Jessie was kneeling on the floor, inspecting the bottom of Benny's pants. "Looks like somebody took the hem up another five inches."

"Are you sure?" Violet hurried over to take a look for herself.

"See?" Jessie lifted the hem. "This isn't the careful stitching that Miss Pennink did yesterday." And Violet agreed.

Benny looked from Jessie to Henry. "You mean somebody played a joke on us?"

"A practical joke," Henry said with a quick nod.

The children heard a gasp and whirled around. It was Miss Pennink standing in the doorway.

"I see Horace has been busy again," she said in a whispery voice.

Jake North suddenly appeared behind Miss Pennink. "What's going on?" he asked. When he caught sight of the pants Henry and Benny were wearing, his dark eyebrows shot up.

Miss Pennink put a hand over her heart. "I simply must sit down," she said.

With some help from Jake, she made her way over to a chair.

"Are you all right, Miss Pennink?" Violet's brown eyes were wide with alarm.

"I just need a moment to recover from the shock, my dear." Miss Pennink smiled a little, but still seemed upset.

Just then, Jessie caught sight of Jake's camera. "Oh, are you here to take more photographs? I could get Gwen if — "

Jake broke in before she could finish. "I just stopped by to see if I left my sunglasses here yesterday," he explained. "But maybe I *will* get a picture of Henry and Benny." And with that, Jake snapped a photo.

It seemed very odd to Jessie. Why would Jake want a picture of them wearing pants that didn't fit?

"So what happened?" Jake asked, his lips curling up into a smile. "Did your pants shrink in the laundry demonstration yesterday?"

"Somebody did this on purpose!" Benny blurted out.

"Yes, indeed," agreed Miss Pennink. "This is Horace's handiwork. He won't put up with it, you know. He just won't stand for this outrage. To be ignored in one's own home is . . . is . . . well, it simply isn't right!"

A little later, when Gwen was pouring Miss Pennink a cup of tea, she said, "You don't really think that, do you, Miss Pennink? You *can't* believe a ghost is responsible for these practical jokes."

Sharon, who was sitting beside Miss Pennink, spoke up first. "We *both* believe it!"

Gwen frowned. "Sharon, please!" She put a basket of blueberry muffins on the table, then turned and gave her younger sister a warning look. "You're not helping matters."

Jake pulled up a chair. "It *is* hard to believe a ghost could be doing these things," he said. "And yet . . ."

The Aldens looked at one another. They all wondered why Jake was so eager to believe the house was haunted.

"There's no such thing as ghosts," said Benny, reaching for a muffin.

"Well, if that's true," replied Sharon, "then there's only one other possibility." And she looked at the Aldens.

"What do you mean?" Henry wanted to know.

Sharon narrowed her green eyes. "Well, it seems to me these practical jokes didn't start until the four of you arrived," she said in an icy voice. "Quite a coincidence, wouldn't you agree?"

"What a terrible thing to say, Sharon!" exclaimed Gwen.

"I'm not accusing anyone," Sharon replied. And she gave her long blond hair a toss. "I'm simply stating the facts."

Violet couldn't believe it. "You think *we're* the copycats?"

"Aren't you forgetting a few things?" Jessie asked, looking Sharon straight in the eye.

"Such as . . . ?"

"Well, for starters, we don't have a key to the farmhouse."

Henry added, "Or a motive."

"Making trouble is all the motive *some* people need," Sharon shot back.

Miss Pennink reached out and put a hand on Sharon's arm. "Please, we mustn't accuse one another. This is Horace's doing. I know because this practical joke is exactly like one Horace played when he was a young boy."

"You've had a shock, Miss Pennink," said Gwen. "Are you sure you want to talk about this?"

Nodding, Miss Pennink took a sip of

tea. "I *must* talk about my great-great-grandfather, since no one else will." She took a breath. "It happened back when Horace wasn't much bigger than Benny. His brother Oscar was about a year younger. As the story goes, Oscar was quite small for his age, and for some reason he'd gotten it into his head that he'd *never* grow any bigger. Well, Horace couldn't bear to see his brother unhappy, so one night he — "

"Shortened his brother's pants?" guessed Benny, who was so interested in the conversation, he still hadn't taken a bite of his muffin.

"That's exactly what he did, Benny!" said Miss Pennink. "In fact, Horace kept this up every night for a week. He shortened those pants a little more every time. They say when Horace was finished, his younger brother was certain he'd sprouted right up! And let me tell you something," she added, "Oscar never worried about his size again."

Henry asked, "Did Oscar ever find out that it was a practical joke?"

"It wasn't until years later that he found

out, Henry," said Miss Pennink. "They say Horace and Oscar had a good laugh over it. Of course, by then Oscar had grown to be every bit the size of his brothers!"

Sharon rubbed her arms. "It gives me a chill to think of Horace going around playing practical jokes all over again."

Nobody said anything for a moment. It was Jake who finally broke the silence. "So that's where they went!" he said.

Everyone looked at him. Then they followed his gaze to the sunglasses on the windowsill.

"I must have put my sunglasses down when I was having a cup of coffee yesterday," Jake told them. "I figured they'd be here or at my uncle Draper's." As the Aldens passed the sunglasses to him, Jake thanked Gwen for the tea, then went on his way.

No sooner had he gone than the bell over the front door jangled as the first visitors arrived. Gwen quickly put the teacups into the sink and rushed away with Sharon. Then Miss Pennink disappeared into the changing room.

"I guess we shouldn't be all *that* surprised," said Henry, who was standing still while Violet lowered the hem on his pants. "About Draper Mills being Jake's uncle, I mean."

"That's true," agreed Jessie, snipping away at the stitching on Benny's pants. "Jake *did* mention that his uncle was a poet."

Benny nodded. "And Draper Mills writes poetry." He took a bite of his blueberry muffin.

"Well, that means we can rule Jake out as a suspect," Henry realized.

But Violet wasn't so sure. She thought about it for a moment and then said, "Hmm."

Benny looked over at Violet. "He was only here last night to visit his uncle," he pointed out.

"That's right," said Henry. "There's no reason for us to suspect him of being the copycat."

"I suppose," said Violet, but she didn't sound convinced.

CHAPTER 8

Putting Two and Two Together

After cooling off in the pond, Henry, Jessie, Violet, and Benny changed into clean shorts and T-shirts, then hurried downstairs. They found Aunt Jane reading the newspaper in the living room in front of a whirling fan. She looked up as they trooped into the room.

"I bet that swim felt good!" she said.

"The swim *did* feel good. And now *I* feel good and hungry!" said Benny.

Aunt Jane laughed. "We'll get supper going in a minute. But first, come and see this." She nodded toward the newspaper on her lap.

"What is it, Aunt Jane?" Violet looked over her aunt's shoulder as they gathered around. "Oh!"

In bold letters that seemed to jump off the page, the headline read, IS THE GHOST OF HORACE WAGNER HAVING THE LAST LAUGH? And just beneath that headline was a picture of Sharon Corkum smiling into the camera.

"Look!" cried Benny. "Sharon's holding up the antique birdcage. And you can see Nester, too."

Jessie nodded. "Jake must have taken that picture just before we got back from lunch yesterday."

Aunt Jane sighed. "Carl Mason isn't going to be pleased with this kind of publicity."

The Aldens understood *why* when Aunt Jane read the article aloud. It was all about the farmhouse sign being moved to the barn and the canary appearing inside the antique birdcage. It finished with an account of Horace Wagner and his practical jokes.

The children looked at one another in dismay. Although they had searched everywhere, they hadn't come up with any clues to help solve the mystery. And now it was too late. They still didn't know who the copycat was, and Gwen could lose her job. Mr. Mason would be sure to see that newspaper article when he got back the next day. And the chances were good he'd blame Gwen for not putting a stop to the practical jokes.

They talked about the mystery as they helped Aunt Jane make a pizza for supper. Violet chopped green peppers and onions. Jessie sliced mushrooms and tomatoes. Henry grated mozzarella cheese and put it in a bowl. Benny stood on a chair at the stove and stirred the tomato sauce. And Aunt Jane shaped the dough.

"It's just unbelievable," said Aunt Jane, who had listened wide-eyed as the children told her all about the latest prank with the too-short pants. "Those practical jokes won't seem very funny if Gwen loses her job."

Violet looked over at Aunt Jane. "Do you really think that could happen?" she asked. Her voice sounded tense.

"There's just no telling what Carl Mason might do," said Aunt Jane as she turned down the heat under the sauce. "But even if Gwen doesn't lose her job, I'm afraid she *will* lose volunteers. Not many people will want to work at the farmhouse if they believe it's haunted."

"Oh!" cried Jessie. "I never thought of that."

"Well, you can bet Gwen's thought about it," said Aunt Jane.

While the pizza was in the oven, Jessie and Violet helped Aunt Jane wash the strawberries for dessert. Benny put plates and napkins on the table. And Henry filled four tall glasses and one cracked pink cup with cold apple cider and put them around the table, too.

"It's a good thing we made an *extra*-large pizza!" Benny said when he had finished his third slice.

Aunt Jane smiled over at the youngest

Alden. "I knew you'd be hungry after putting in a full day's work, Benny."

"And we worked *very* hard today, too," Benny told her as he wiped tomato sauce from his chin. "Henry and I made ice cream the old-fashioned way. The visitors helped, too. They turned the crank on the ice-cream freezer around and around." He looked over at his aunt. "And you know what else?"

"What?" Aunt Jane smiled as she dished up the strawberries. She was eager to hear all about their day.

"Everybody had a chance to sample the ice cream!" said Benny.

Henry couldn't keep from laughing. "I think you had more than one sample, Benny!"

"Jessie and I helped out with Miss Pennink's workshop," Violet put in. "We were showing how old clothing was recycled during the Victorian era."

Jessie knew Violet would be too shy to say anything, so she spoke up for her. "Some of the older kids didn't want to make a braided rag rug or a rag doll. So Violet showed them how to make a rag octopus — like the one Mrs. McGregor made for her sister. It was such a big hit, Gwen's going to include it in the workshops from now on."

"I tore some of the old clothing into long strips," Benny reminded them.

"Yes, and that was very helpful," Violet told him.

Aunt Jane nodded. "I'm sure Gwen appreciates all the help you children have given her."

"I just wish we could solve the mystery of the copycat," said Henry as he ate his strawberries. "That would *really* help Gwen."

Aunt Jane reached for an envelope that was on top of the refrigerator. "You left your photographs on the table this morning," she said, handing the envelope to Violet. "Weren't you planning on showing them to Gwen?"

Violet nodded. "I forgot all about them. I'll try to remember tomorrow."

"I love the photo taken in the farmhouse office," said Aunt Jane as she sat down.

Violet flipped through the photos. "Which one do you mean, Aunt Jane?"

"I bet it's the one Gwen took of us in our Victorian clothes," guessed Jessie.

Aunt Jane smiled when Violet held it up. "Yes, that's it!"

"We should put that one in the Alden family album," suggested Benny. "Don't you think so, Violet?"

But Violet didn't answer. She was staring hard at the picture. Something about it bothered her. But she didn't know what it was. Finally she gave a little shrug and tucked the snapshot back into the envelope.

"Don't you think so, Violet?" Benny said again, a little louder this time. "Don't you think that one should go in the Alden family album?"

Violet looked up in surprise. "Oh, yes! That's exactly where it should go. It will always remind us of our trip back in time."

"And the mystery of the copycat," added Henry.

While they cleared the table after dinner, the Aldens still talked about the mystery.

"It's funny," said Benny. "The practical joke with Nester was just like the thaumatrope." He carried the empty glasses over to the sink. "First there *wasn't* a bird in the cage, and then there *was*."

Jessie nodded. "There's one difference, though. The canary in the antique bird-cage wasn't an optical illusion. Neither were those shortened pants."

"But they *were* tricks," said Henry, stacking the plates on the counter.

"You know, I've been thinking about Sharon," said Jessie. "It's funny she didn't find the birdcage until Jake arrived with his camera."

Violet turned off the tap. She told the others how she had caught a glimpse of burrs on Sharon's socks the day the sign disappeared. "Benny said there were weeds behind the barn where he found the sign. Right?" She turned to her younger brother.

"I guess that *is* suspicious," Benny said uncertainly. "But maybe Sharon was just out gathering wildflowers and that's where those burrs came from."

"That's a possibility, Benny," said Jessie as she slipped the dessert spoons into the soapy water. "I don't think we can rule Sharon out as a suspect, though. I know she was nice to you yesterday, but I still don't trust her. She could have taken Gwen's keys to get into the farmhouse and then set up the practical jokes."

Henry agreed. "And I'm sure she's heard plenty about Horace and his practical jokes from Miss Pennink."

"Sharon's so hard to figure out," Benny said, carefully drying his cracked pink cup. "She was nice at first. But then she got angry."

Jessie nodded. "Her whole attitude changed as soon as Gwen mentioned we'd be working at the farmhouse."

"Gwen mentioned something else, too," Henry reminded them. "She said we were good at solving mysteries."

"Oh!" cried Violet, rinsing the soapy dishes. "You think that's why Sharon was acting so weird?"

Henry shrugged. "If she *is* the copycat,

she sure wouldn't want *us* snooping around."

"What I can't figure out," Violet went on, "is why Sharon would *want* everyone to think the house is haunted."

"Maybe she's trying to get even with Gwen," Jessie guessed.

Violet thought about this. "You mean because of the fashion shows?"

"It's a possibility," said Jessie.

"But her sister's job is on the line!" Violet looked startled. "I can't believe Sharon would do anything to hurt Gwen like that." It was too awful to think about.

"It's hard to believe, Violet," said Jessie. "But you heard how angry she was at the ice-cream parlor last night. And she did tell Gwen she'd be sorry."

"You know," said Henry, "Sharon isn't the only suspect. There's somebody else we might want to include on that list."

"You're thinking of Draper Mills, right?" guessed Jessie.

Henry nodded. "It seems odd that he was at the farmhouse so early yesterday morning."

Violet turned to face Henry. "Well, he *does* do repairs around the house."

"I know," said Henry, nodding. "But Gwen seemed surprised when he said he was fixing a window shade."

Benny looked thoughtful. "She didn't know any of the shades needed fixing."

"And Draper was acting very nervous," added Jessie. "Did you notice?"

Henry and Benny nodded. They'd picked up on this, too.

"Draper isn't comfortable around people," Violet was quick to remind them. "Gwen and Aunt Jane both told us that. Just because he was acting nervous, that doesn't make him suspicious." Violet was shy, and being around a lot of people made her nervous, too.

"That's true, Violet," Jessie said quietly as she put the clean spoons away in a drawer. "But we can't be sure he wasn't getting things set up yesterday morning for the practical joke. We have to consider every possibility. Draper *was* in the right place at the right time."

Benny had something to add. "Maybe Draper moved the sign, too. He doesn't like anybody stopping at the farm."

Violet looked at Benny, then over at Jessie and Henry. She could see they believed it was possible. "Draper *is* afraid his flowers will get trampled. That's a reason for moving the sign, but why would he play those practical jokes with the canary and the shortened pants?"

"To convince everyone the house is haunted," Henry said. "Maybe he's hoping it'll keep people away."

Jessie handed Violet the pizza platter to wash. "And Draper does have his own set of keys."

Benny added, "I bet he knows a lot about the Wagner family. After all, he's worked on the farm for a long time."

"I suppose it's possible," Violet admitted reluctantly. She didn't like to be suspicious just because someone was nervous.

"I just thought of something else," Henry said. "There's one other person with keys to the farmhouse. And this person knows more about Horace Wagner than anybody else does."

Jessie looked puzzled. So did Violet and Benny.

"Who is it?" they all said at the same time.

"Miss Pennink," answered Henry.

"Miss Pennink!" The others were so surprised by this, all they could do was stare in disbelief.

"Oh, you don't really suspect Miss Pennink, do you, Henry?" said Violet.

"I don't want to think she would do something like that, Violet," he told her. "But we have to consider everybody. And I heard she sometimes opens the house early in the morning if Gwen has a meeting in town with Mr. Mason. So she must have her own keys."

They had to admit that it was possible. Wasn't Miss Pennink upset because her great-great-grandfather was being ignored by Carl Mason? And hadn't Miss Pennink told them that one way or another she'd make sure people knew about Horace Wagner? What better way than by playing his practical jokes all over again?

"But which one is the copycat?" Benny wondered aloud. "Miss Pennink, Draper Mills, or Sharon?"

"I think we should include Jake North on our list of suspects," said Violet.

Benny looked confused. "But Draper Mills is Jake's uncle, remember? That means Jake had a good reason for being at the farmhouse last night."

"I know," Violet said. "Except . . ."

Jessie asked, "What is it, Violet?"

"Well, it also means that Jake could've borrowed Draper's keys!" said Violet. "And his uncle probably has told him all about Horace and his practical jokes."

"Good point," said Henry.

Benny was deep in thought. "You don't think . . ." he said, and then stopped himself.

"Are you wondering if the farmhouse

might really be haunted?" Violet asked in a gentle voice. Then she quickly added, "I don't blame you, Benny. I've wondered about that myself."

Benny turned to Jessie. "Do *you* believe it's haunted?"

Jessie didn't answer right away. Finally, she said, "No, I don't."

"Now that I think about it," Violet put in, "I'm sure it isn't." She wasn't really sure, but she wanted Benny to believe she was.

Benny looked up at his older brother. "What do you say, Henry?"

"There's no such thing as ghosts, Benny," Henry told him firmly.

"I didn't think so," Benny said, looking relieved. And then he added, "But I can't help wondering what's going to happen next."

"I have a feeling we won't have to wait long to find out!" declared Jessie.

CHAPTER 9

What's Wrong with This Picture?

Miss Pennink breathed a sigh of relief when Henry and Benny came out of the changing room the next morning. "Looks like Horace decided not to shorten those pants again," she said. "Thank goodness for that!" Then, after a moment's thought, she added, "But we must be on our guard. Horace might have left his mark somewhere else."

Jessie was hurrying off with Violet to get the farmhouse ready for the day. "Don't worry, Miss Pennink," she said. "We'll keep an eye out for any more practical jokes."

Jessie and Violet did just that as they went from one room to another, lifting shades and opening windows. "So far, so good," said Violet, coming out of the study.

Jessie nodded. "The last thing Gwen needs today is another practical joke."

"I was hoping my snapshots would cheer her up a bit," remarked Violet. "But . . ." Her words trailed away in a sigh.

Stepping into the parlor, Violet stopped so suddenly that her older sister almost bumped into her. Then Jessie realized what was wrong — all the family portraits were facing the wrong way. Somebody had hung them up backward!

Jessie and Violet stood frozen to the spot. They couldn't believe their eyes! Finally, they ran to the office and told everyone of their discovery.

"The pictures really *are* backward," said Benny as he peered into the shadowy parlor.

Sharon turned to Miss Pennink in surprise. "Horace *did* leave his mark again."

"I wish there were some other explanation." Miss Pennink sat down on the front staircase in the entrance hall. "But there's no doubt in my mind. This has Horace's name all over it."

"Unless I miss my guess," said Gwen, "Horace once played a practical joke just like this one. Am I right, Miss Pennink?"

The elderly woman nodded slowly as she began to tell them about her great-great-grandfather's practical joke with the backward pictures. "Horace had a good friend named Tom Brankin," she said. "When Tom was turned down for membership in a fancy Elmford club, Horace was so angry he decided to give this club a taste of its own medicine."

Benny's eyes were huge. "What did Horace do?"

"He applied for membership himself," Miss Pennink went on. "Of course the club was delighted. Horace, you see, was highly regarded in the community. When the membership committee paid a visit to the Wagner home, they discovered the portraits on the walls and the pictures on the piano were facing the wrong way. I believe," Miss Pennink added, "the pictures on the piano are probably facing the wrong way now, too."

They all crowded around the parlor doorway to check it out. Sure enough, the pictures in fancy frames on the piano had indeed been turned around.

Miss Pennink continued. "They say Horace enjoyed the look of surprise on the faces of that membership committee. They had no idea what the backward pictures meant, of course. At least not until the next day. That's when Horace sent them a note."

"What did it say?" Sharon asked in a hushed voice. "The note, I mean."

Miss Pennink smiled a little. "It said that Horace was turning his back on their little club, the same way they had turned their backs on his good friend Tom Brankin."

"Oh, I get it!" said Benny. "That's why the pictures were turned away from everyone."

"Exactly," said Miss Pennink. "And now the entire Wagner family have turned their backs on those who have ignored Horace. Carl Mason, for one."

When Gwen noticed Draper trimming the hedge out front, she asked him to step inside. He looked into the parlor and shook his head.

"How could such a thing happen?" he asked.

"I wish I knew," said Gwen. "Did you see anything suspicious last night, Draper?"

Draper Mills gave his head a firm shake. "Not a thing."

At that moment, the door opened again. It was Carl Mason, and he had a rolled-up newspaper in his hand. "Miss Corkum, if you thought I'd approve of this publicity stunt," he said, holding up the paper, "then you're in for a surprise!"

Jessie and Henry exchanged glances. Carl Mason seemed to think the practical jokes were Gwen's idea.

"I can assure you, Mr. Mason, this is not a publicity stunt," Gwen said quietly. "And you might as well know, the practical jokes haven't ended yet."

As Gwen showed the museum curator into the parlor, Henry, Jessie, Violet, and Benny went off to check the house for any sign of forced entry. But once again, it was clear the copycat must have had a key to get inside. Finally they went upstairs to make sure the copycat hadn't pulled any more pranks.

After a careful search, Violet said, "Nothing looks out of place up here." And the others agreed.

Just before heading downstairs again, Jessie glanced through a bedroom window and caught sight of a red sports car coming up the driveway. "How strange," she said.

"What's strange?" asked Henry.

"Have you noticed how Jake North always arrives at just the right time?"

"What do you mean?"

"I mean, at the right time to take a photograph of the latest practical joke."

Henry glanced out the window. When he spotted Jake, he said, "Now that you mention it . . ."

"Do you think it's more than a coincidence?" asked Violet as she joined her older brother and sister at the window. Benny was close behind.

"A lot more!" replied Jessie.

"It does seem odd," agreed Benny.

Violet watched for a moment as Jake North strolled across the front lawn, his camera hanging from a strap around his neck. When he removed his sunglasses and tucked them into his shirt pocket, Violet's eyes got very large.

Henry said, "What's the matter, Violet?"

Violet didn't answer. Instead, she snapped her fingers and went racing away. She returned a few moments later with a photograph. It was the one Gwen had taken of the Aldens in their Victorian costumes. "I knew there was something funny about this picture," she said softly. "But I couldn't put my finger on it until now."

Jessie glanced at the photo. "I don't understand. It's just a picture of the four of us standing in the office."

"Yes," said Violet. "But it was taken the day Jake *said* he left his sunglasses here."

"He *did* leave them." Henry looked puzzled. "They were on the — " Suddenly catching on, Henry drew in his breath. "Jake's sunglasses!"

"How come they're not on the windowsill in this picture?" asked Benny, trying to keep his voice low.

"That's exactly what I'm wondering," said Violet. "Jake was gone before this picture was taken."

"Which means he left his sunglasses on the windowsill *after* the farmhouse had closed for the day!" concluded Jessie.

"You think Jake North is the copycat?" asked Benny in surprise.

Violet nodded. "I'm sure of it."

Henry took a deep breath. "Jake North has some explaining to do." And he led the way downstairs.

"I thought I'd made myself quite clear, Mr. North." Mr. Mason was pointing to the front page of the newspaper. He sounded upset. "This type of article isn't what I had in mind when I invited you out here."

"It's my job to report the facts, Mr. Mason," argued Jake. "And the facts point to this farmhouse being haunted."

"What are you doing here, Jake?" demanded Henry, who was edging his way past Miss Pennink on the staircase. "Why *now*, I mean?"

Jake looked startled by the question. "Well . . . uh . . . Miss Pennink was a bit under the weather yesterday. I thought I'd find out how she was feeling today. Is there anything wrong with that?"

"Are you sure you aren't here to take a picture?" asked Jessie.

"A picture?" echoed Jake. "A picture of what?"

"Of the latest practical joke."

"What do you mean?" Jake inquired. "Has something else happened?"

"You should know," Benny blurted out, his hands on his hips. "After all, you set it up. Didn't you?"

Jake laughed. "You're kidding. Right?"

Even Mr. Mason looked puzzled. "What's going on? Surely you're not hinting that

Jake North had anything to do with these practical jokes?"

Benny nodded vigorously. "Jake had plenty to do with them!"

"He sure did," added Jessie, watching Jake closely.

Violet started to say, "And we can prove — "

But Jake interrupted. "I have no idea what you're talking about." His eyes shifted. "You kids are getting all worked up about nothing."

Violet stepped forward. "You said you left your sunglasses at the farmhouse the day of the laundry demonstration. Remember?"

"Of course I remember. They were on the windowsill. What's that got to do with anything?"

"If that's true," finished Violet, "then why aren't they on the windowsill in this snapshot?" And she held the photograph up for Jake to see. "This was taken just before the farmhouse closed that day."

Jake shrugged. "That doesn't mean a

thing. The photo was probably taken some other time."

"I remember this snapshot." Gwen was studying it closely. "I took it myself, and it *was* the day of the laundry demonstration. You'd left hours before this picture was taken, Jake. And yet . . . your sunglasses were on the windowsill the next morning. How do you explain that?"

Draper Mills looked at his nephew. "Jake, what's this all about?"

Carl Mason examined the photograph, then passed it on to Jake. "I would certainly like to hear what you have to say, Mr. North. And remember, a picture's worth a thousand words."

Jake stared at the photo for what seemed like ages. He opened his mouth several times, then closed it again. Finally his shoulders slumped. "Yes, I admit it," he said. "I copied Horace Wagner's practical jokes. I . . . I wanted everyone to think the farmhouse was haunted."

Miss Pennink's mouth dropped open. Gwen and Sharon both stared wide-eyed.

"But why?" Draper Mills demanded, looking completely bewildered. "Why would you do such a thing, Jake?"

Henry knew the answer to that one. "You wanted something interesting to write about, didn't you?"

Jake nodded. "We're supposed to submit a few newspaper articles when we go back to college. I knew what I'd written so far would put my teachers to sleep. I just wanted a scoop, and there certainly wasn't much chance of getting *that* in Elmford." Jake paused. "I got the idea for a haunted house story when the farmhouse sign disappeared. In fact, I was planning to write a whole series of articles on the ghostly practical jokes. I asked my uncle about Horace Wagner, and he told me everything I needed to know."

"You said it was for background information," protested Draper. "I had no idea. . . ."

Jessie looked accusingly at Jake. "The truth is, you wanted to find out about the practical jokes so you could copy them."

Jake didn't deny it. "I knew there was going to be a laundry demonstration, and when I heard about Horace hiding a gift in the laundry tub, I couldn't resist. I drove out of town, bought a canary, then came back to the farm to have dinner with Uncle Draper." Jake avoided looking his uncle in the eye. "I knew my uncle was in the habit of nodding off for a while after supper. I just waited for my chance and — "

"You took the keys," finished Violet. "Then you slipped into the farmhouse, put the canary in the antique birdcage, and hid the cage in the empty laundry tub."

"The next night, you shortened our pants," concluded Henry.

"I'm not handy with a needle and thread," admitted Jake, "but I figured Horace probably wasn't, either."

"Only you made a mistake," offered Violet. "You left your sunglasses behind."

Jake corrected her. "No, I did that on purpose. My sunglasses gave me an excuse to come back the next morning. That way, I could get a snapshot of Henry and Benny wearing those pants." Jake sighed. "I can't believe the sunglasses were the one thing that did me in. I didn't count on you Aldens being such good detectives."

"And you did this, too?" asked Miss Pennink, gesturing toward the parlor.

Jake nodded sheepishly.

"You did it all, then," stated Gwen. "The sign, the canary, the — "

Jake broke in, "Everything *except* the sign. I had nothing to do with that."

"Then who . . . ?" asked Gwen.

"It was me." Sharon's face turned red. "I was the one who moved the sign. I had no idea it would cause so many problems." She sat down on the staircase next to Miss Pennink. "I knew a photographer was coming out from the Elmford newspaper that day, and I figured it would be good for my modeling career to get my picture in the paper."

"So you moved the sign hoping that Jake would have trouble finding the farmhouse," Henry guessed.

Sharon nodded. "I just wanted to delay things until I got back from the dentist."

She turned to her sister. "I was planning to put the sign right back."

"That's how you got burrs on your socks, isn't it?" said Violet.

Sharon looked over at Violet in surprise. "You really are good detectives," she said. "That *is* how I got the burrs. Everything's overgrown behind the old barn."

Gwen let out a sigh. "I can't believe you'd do something like that."

"I'm really sorry, Gwen." Sharon hung her head.

Miss Pennink spoke up next. "I should have known it wasn't my great-great-grandfather. Horace Wagner's jokes were *never* meant to hurt anyone."

"I never meant to hurt anyone, either," Jake said, almost as if he were trying to convince himself. "After all, it *was* good publicity for the farmhouse. Wasn't it?"

Jessie frowned. "Gwen almost lost her job."

Jake looked at the ground. "I'm sorry, Gwen," he apologized. "I had no idea your job was at risk."

"There's no danger of Miss Corkum losing her job," Mr. Mason told Jake. "I was the one who invited you out here in the first place. I'm afraid that was *my* mistake."

Jake looked over at his uncle. "I know I betrayed your trust, Uncle Draper. But I give you my word, I'll make things right."

Looking sad and disappointed, Draper Mills headed for the door. With a hand on the doorknob, he turned to his nephew. "Right now your word doesn't mean much to me," he said, and then he was gone.

When Jake finally spoke again, he sounded truly sorry. "I *will* fix things. I'll write another article for the newspaper. Everyone will know that the Wagner farmhouse *isn't* haunted."

"That's a good start, young man," Mr. Mason told him. "A very good start."

CHAPTER 10

April Fool Pie

When the Aldens finished their last day as tour guides, Aunt Jane invited everyone over for a special barbecue. Jessie and Benny sat on one side of an extra-long picnic table, along with Mr. Mason, Aunt Jane, Gwen, and Sharon. Across from them sat Henry, Violet, Miss Pennink, Draper Mills, and Jake North.

"These are the best hamburgers I've had in a long time," declared Jake, who had been true to his word. A big article had appeared in the newspaper that morning. It said that the old Wagner farmhouse wasn't haunted and never had been.

"I'm glad you could make it, Jake," Aunt Jane said with a warm smile. "I didn't know if you'd be too busy at work."

"Oh, this was my day off." Jake wiped some mustard from the corner of his mouth. "I'm lucky to even have a job after the stunts I've pulled. It's on a trial basis, of course — which is more than I deserve."

Draper Mills put a hand on his nephew's shoulder. "Everyone deserves a second chance."

"Yes, indeed," agreed Mr. Mason. "We all make mistakes. It's learning from them that matters. It happens to be one of the reasons I enjoy history so much. We can learn from the past and hopefully not repeat the same mistakes." Mr. Mason cleared his throat. "I'm ashamed to say I've been guilty of some rigid thinking, the sort of thinking that was common in the Victorian era. I should have known better. Ever since that article about Horace came out in the newspaper, the museum's been flooded with

calls. People want to know more about Horace and about the history of Elmford. If he can spark that kind of interest, Horace Wagner's okay with me. And I have a feeling," he added, "that Miss Pennink's book will be sold out in Elmford."

"You wrote a book, Miss Pennink?" cried Gwen. "You never said a word."

Miss Pennink beamed. "It's a history of the Wagner family."

The Aldens looked at one another. That was what Miss Pennink had meant about making sure everyone knew about Horace Wagner.

"I've kept it a secret," Miss Pennink went on, "knowing how Mr. Mason felt about Horace and his practical jokes. I didn't want to risk Draper's job. You see, Draper's helping me. As soon as I finish a chapter, Draper goes over it and makes suggestions. Every morning, he leaves his notes for me in the pantry — in a crock pot."

Gwen winked at Draper Mills. "That explains why you were in the farmhouse so early that morning. I didn't think any of the window shades needed fixing."

Draper nodded. "You caught me by surprise. Sorry for not being more honest."

"It's really quite a delightful book," said Mr. Mason. "Miss Pennink told me about it the day I put Horace's photograph back where it belonged."

"I'm afraid I've been guilty of some rigid thinking myself." Gwen put an arm around her younger sister. "I'm sure we can work something out, Sharon. There's no reason you shouldn't take part in those fashion shows."

Sharon's face lit up. "Oh, do you mean it?"

Gwen nodded. "It's a good way for you to find out if modeling is what you really want." Then she added, "I was thinking that the farmhouse gardens would be a wonderful place to hold some of those fashion shows. And who knows? Maybe Victorian dresses could be modeled along with the modern ones."

Sharon was thrilled. "That's a great idea!"

Benny had a question. He hesitated for a moment, then blurted out, "Sharon, why didn't you want us working at the farm-house?"

Gwen's sister lowered her eyes. "I'm sorry for being so unfriendly," she said. "The truth is, I was glad we were going to be shorthanded at the farmhouse. I thought it'd give me a chance to prove to my sister that I was responsible enough to handle any situation — including taking part in the fashion shows. When I heard you were volunteering, I thought my chance to prove myself was gone." Sharon took a breath. "I never should have accused you of setting up those practical jokes," she said, looking at each of the Aldens in turn. "Because of you, my sister still has her job."

Draper Mills had a confession to make, too. "I haven't been very friendly, either. It's no secret I didn't take kindly to the farm being opened up to the public. I thought all those visitors would trample all over the garden. But folks have been great. It's been a nice surprise."

"Well," said Aunt Jane, "we're certainly not short on reasons to celebrate today!"

Miss Pennink agreed. "It's a good thing I made a very special dessert."

Benny grinned. "Dessert?"

"Wait right here," Miss Pennink told him, then she disappeared into the kitchen. Returning a moment later, she said, "This was my great-great-grandfather's favorite dessert — April Fool pie!"

"April Fool pie?" echoed Benny. "What's that?"

Miss Pennink set the dessert on the picnic table. "You won't know until you try it, Benny." And she gave him the first piece.

"It looks like apple pie," observed Benny. "Mmmm, it tastes like apple pie, too!"

"April Fool!" said Miss Pennink with a big smile. "There isn't a single apple in it. It's made with crackers and a mixture of water, lemon juice, sugar, and a teaspoon of cream of tartar. You sprinkle it with cinnamon and bake it in the oven. And that's how you get — "

"April Fool pie!" everyone cried out.

Jessie said, "This is a perfect way to end the week."

"And our trip back in time," added Violet.

"We even solved a mystery on our trip," declared Benny. "Right, Henry?"

"Like I said before, Benny," Henry answered, "some things never change!"

GERTRUDE CHANDLER WARNER discovered when she was teaching that many readers who like an exciting story could find no books that were both easy and fun to read. She decided to try to meet this need, and her first book, *The Boxcar Children*, quickly proved she had succeeded.

Miss Warner drew on her own experiences to write the mystery. As a child she spent hours watching trains go by on the tracks opposite her family home. She often dreamed about what it would be like to set up housekeeping in a caboose or freight car — the situation the Alden children find themselves in.

When Miss Warner received requests for more adventures involving Henry, Jessie, Violet, and Benny Alden, she began additional stories. In each, she chose a special setting and introduced unusual or eccentric characters who liked the unpredictable.

While the mystery element is central to each of Miss Warner's books, she never thought of them as strictly juvenile mysteries. She liked to stress the Aldens' independence and resourcefulness and their solid New England devotion to using up and making do. The Aldens go about most of their adventures with as little adult supervision as possible — something else that delights young readers.

Miss Warner lived in Putnam, Connecticut, until her death in 1979. During her lifetime, she received hundreds of letters from girls and boys telling her how much they liked her books.